Dial-a-Croc

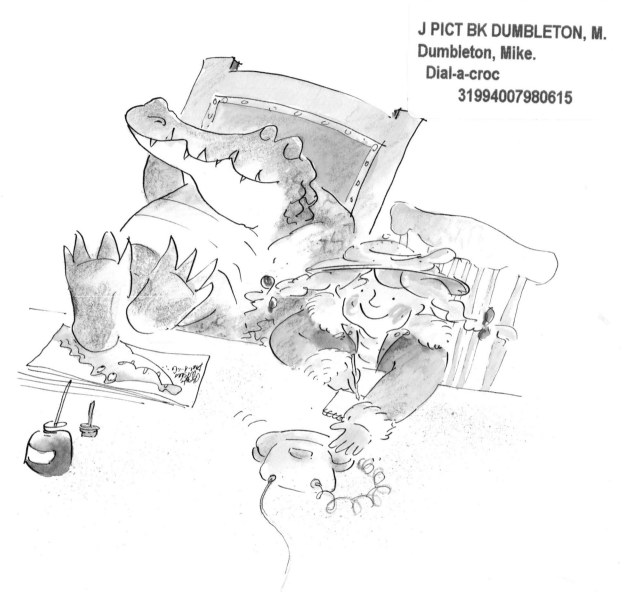

by Mike Dumbleton

illustrated by Ann James

ORCHARD BOOKS   NEW YORK

For Jay, Luke, and Nathan,
and the real Vanessa
—M.D.

For Freya the Intrepid
—A.J.

Text copyright © 1991 by Mike Dumbleton
Illustrations copyright © 1991 by Ann James
First American Edition 1991 published by Orchard Books
First published in Australia by Omnibus Books

Orchard Books, A division of Franklin Watts, Inc., 387 Park Avenue South, New York, NY 10016

Printed in Hong Kong   10   9   8   7   6   5   4   3   2   1

Library of Congress Cataloging-in-Publication Data
Dumbleton, Mike. Dial-a-croc/Mike Dumbleton; illustrated by Ann James.—
1st American ed.   p.   cm.
Summary: Vanessa makes a lot of money when she captures a crocodile in the Australian
outback and gets him to work for her until the crocodile becomes homesick.
ISBN 0-531-05945-6.   ISBN 0-531-08545-7 (lib.)
[1. Crocodiles—Fiction. 2. Australia—Fiction.]   I. James, Ann, ill.
II. Title.   PZ7.D89355Di   1991   [E]—dc20   90-25385

One morning Vanessa awakened with
a brilliant idea for making money.

She put on her jungle jeans, her hunting jacket,
and her wide-brimmed hat.

She stuffed her bullwhip, camping
knife, and trapping net into her
shoulder bag.

Then she rolled up her sleeping bag
and reached for a book called
How To Catch Fierce Animals.

Out in the outback, beyond the Back of Beyond,
Vanessa found what she was looking for—

a dangerous, toothy,
rough, tough
CROCODILE.

After she trapped him with her net,
she said, "You have a choice.
You can be ten handbags
and five pairs of shoes,
or you can help me make lots of money."

"I'll take the money," said the crocodile at last,
and they shook on it, hand and claw.

Just to be safe, Vanessa
tied up the crocodile's jaw with her bullwhip.
Then she rode him home,
all the way from beyond the Back of Beyond.

The next day Vanessa put an
advertisement in the newspaper.

DIAL-A-CROC
We get our teeth into anything.
No job too small.
Payment by the hour.
Phone 81205.

Dial-a-Croc's first job
was in the House of Horrors.

He was so frightening that
the owners had to put up a new sign.

They sold ten times the usual number of tickets. Vanessa and Dial-a-Croc started to make lots of money.

Their next job was at the Olympic Swimming Pool.
"I want my team to swim faster,"
explained the coach.

Dial-a-Croc smiled.
"If I catch them, may I eat them?" he whispered to Vanessa.
"No!" she hissed. "Remember the handbags,
and do as you're told."

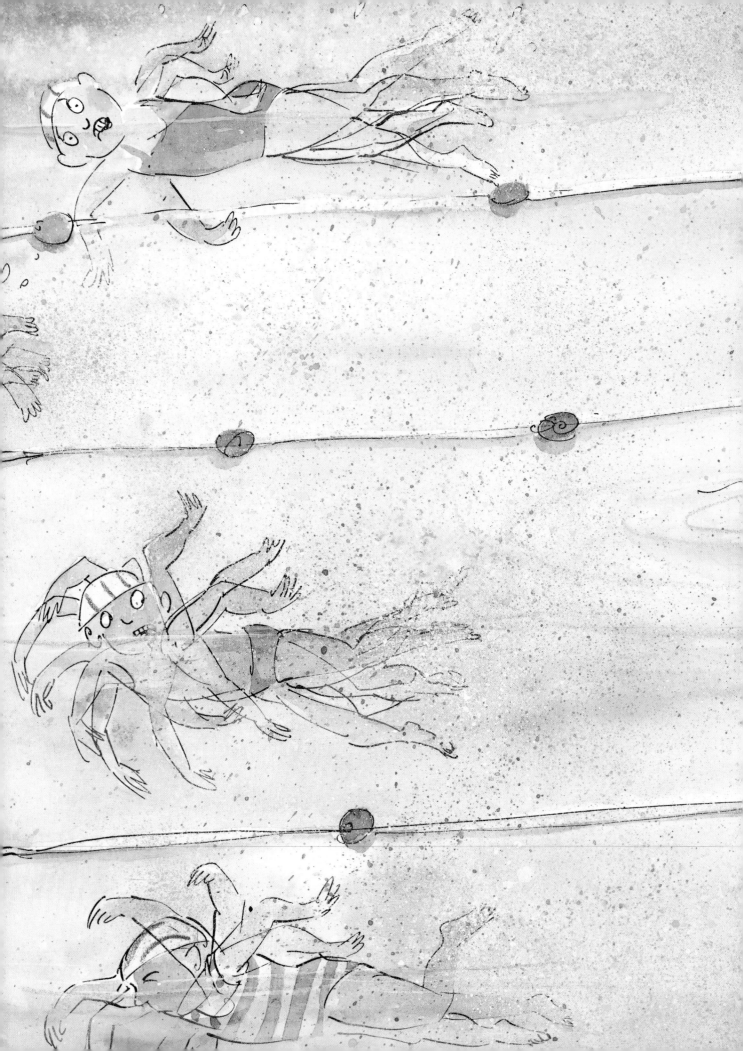

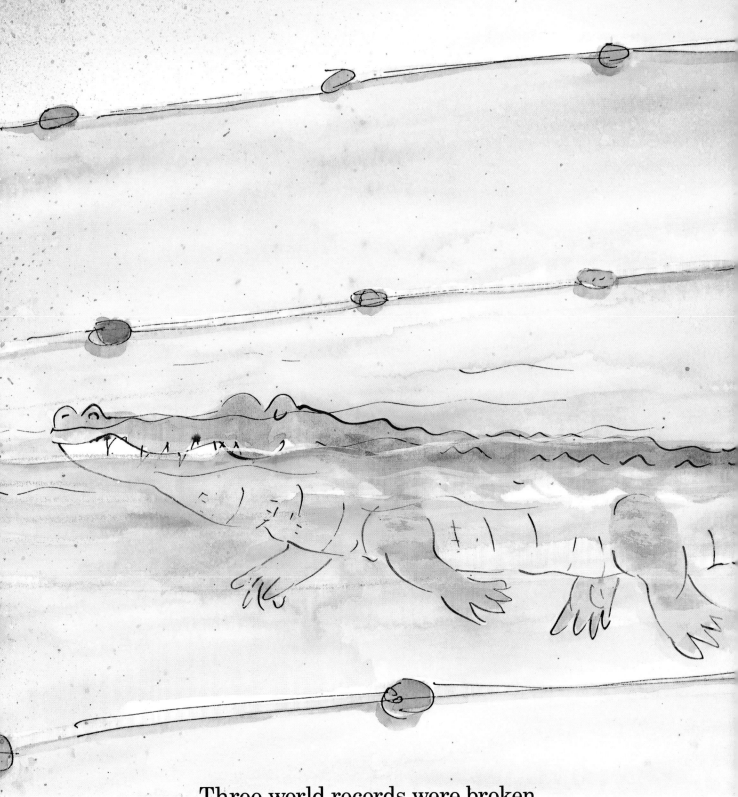

Three world records were broken.

Vanessa bought a car with a phone for herself
and a special trailer for Dial-a-Croc.

"You'll be a crocodile in style," she said.

The phone never stopped ringing.

At the Chunky Chewing Gum factory,
Dial-a-Croc was the best chewing gum checker
they had ever had!

He worked at the railway station
in the rush hour, punching tickets
twenty at a time.

In the Eskimo Cool factory he was an ice crusher.

He was called in to rescue
people in accidents.

Vanessa bought herself a house
with a crocodile-shaped swimming pool,
and she bought Dial-a-Croc an expensive waterproof
watch guaranteed to a depth of one hundred yards.

"I think it suits me," he said proudly.
"So do I," Vanessa agreed.

Dial-a-Croc appeared on television,
advertising toothpaste.
He sang:

"Save your teeth, big or tiny.
Keep them clean, bright, and shiny.
Brush decay away today.
Then you can smile like me, okay?

Soon he was famous.
Everyone wanted his autograph.
He was a regular guest on game shows,
and he opened wildlife reserves.

Once he appeared on a talk show and happily discussed
life in the outback, beyond the Back of Beyond.
But for the first time Vanessa noticed
a faraway sadness in his eyes.

To make Dial-a-Croc's life happier,
Vanessa bought him a helicopter.
"No more traffic jams," she promised.
"You'll have extra time to relax."
"Now I'm really going up in the world," he replied.

But the more famous Dial-a-Croc grew, the sadder and more faraway the look in his eyes became.

Vanessa was worried.

One morning Vanessa awakened to find Dial-a-Croc by her bed.
"You have a choice," he said.
"You can be my breakfast with toast and jam,
or you can take me home to my friends."
"Whatever I decide," said Vanessa, "life just won't be the same."

"I'll take you home," Vanessa agreed at last.
"Besides, you wouldn't want to eat me.
I taste worse than cold cabbage."

Out in the outback, beyond the Back of Beyond,
Vanessa and Dial-a-Croc hugged each other
and said good-bye.

Then Dial-a-Croc gave Vanessa a present.
"It's something to remember me by," he said.

Vanessa opened it and smiled.
Inside she found . . .

. . . shoes and a handbag to match—
mock crocodile, of course.